THE CASE OF THE MISSING TREASURE

A MURDER
MOST UNLADYLIKE
MINI
MYSTERY

ROBIN STEVENS

PUFFIN

PUFFIN BOOKS

UK | USA | Canada | Ireland | Australia
India | New Zealand | South Africa

Puffin Books is part of the Penguin Random House group of companies
whose addresses can be found at global.penguinrandomhouse.com.

www.penguin.co.uk
www.puffin.co.uk
www.ladybird.co.uk

First published 2018
This edition published 2019

003

Text copyright © Robin Stevens, 2018
Cover copyright © Nina Tara, 2018

The moral right of the author and illustrator has been asserted

Set in 12.5/18 pt New Baskerville Std
Typeset by Jouve (UK), Milton Keynes
Printed and bound in Great Britain by Clays Ltd, Elcograf S.p.A.

A CIP catalogue record for this book is available from the British Library

ISBN: 978–0–241–39554–7

All correspondence to:
Puffin Books
Penguin Random House Children's
80 Strand, London WC2R 0RL

To booksellers. You're absolute heroes.

THE CASE OF THE MISSING TREASURE

Being an account of

The Case of the Cursed Mummy.
Written by Daisy Wells,
Detective Society President, aged 15.

Begun 30th May 1936, concerning
exciting events that took place on
Saturday 9th May 1936.

My Secretary and Vice-President Hazel is busy writing the story of our seventh murder case. It is taking her a long time, because it was such an excellent mystery. We have faced plenty of dastardly murderers in our careers to date, but I believe we have seldom come up against such a cunning crime.

Hazel tells me that I always say that. Perhaps I do. Or perhaps the criminals we meet are becoming cleverer.

Nevertheless, we are better detectives with every new case. It is now almost impossible to outwit us – or at least no one has managed it yet.

So, while Hazel is writing away, I, the Honourable Daisy Wells, have decided to give an account of another mystery we faced in recent weeks. It was very exciting, and very heroic, and I was very brilliant and brave (Hazel and our friends George and Alexander helped too). We caught criminals, and recovered treasure, and really everyone in England should be grateful to us.

Although I do not think I need any more introduction, Hazel insists upon it. So: I am Daisy Wells, and my best friend Hazel Wong and I are the two most important members of the Detective Society, an organization which is famous on at least two continents. One day we will own the world's finest consulting detective agency, although at the moment we are still forced to struggle through our schooldays as though we were ordinary children.

We are currently on our way back to Deepdean School for Girls, although (very pleasingly) we have not been there much this year. For reasons that I shall let Hazel's other casebooks tell you about, we have spent this spring first in Hong Kong, and then in London. In London we were staying with my Uncle Felix and his new wife, whom we have been told to call Aunt Lucy.

Because of his utterly secret and extremely important job, Uncle Felix is not exactly a *usual* sort of uncle, nor is Aunt Lucy an ordinary aunt, and so living in their flat is fascinating. There are mysteries everywhere, and we encountered our first only a few days after our arrival in London.

We were sitting round the breakfast table on Wednesday morning, and Bridget had just brought in the morning papers. Bridget is supposed to be Aunt Lucy and Uncle Felix's maid, but, like every other part of Uncle Felix and Aunt Lucy's life, she is rather unusual. She can read coded messages as quickly as I can read English, and when she answers the telephone I have heard her speak at least six different languages. I suppose it is clever of Uncle Felix to use her for other purposes, for who really pays attention to a maid?

'There's been another one, Mr M,' Bridget said to Uncle Felix, dropping the pile of newspapers on the table next to the butter dish. 'Sir John Soane's Museum this time!'

'Another what?' I asked, on the alert. I could see that Hazel was sitting up too. I peered at the paper on the top of the pile:

Sneak Thief Strikes Again

Yesterday morning the curators at Sir John Soane's Museum were horrified to discover the theft of several of their most precious Greek and Roman artefacts. A window was smashed, the cases themselves lay open and the items, including a small bust and a gold necklace, were missing. This is the tenth such theft in the last month, but only the second to leave behind such destruction. In many of the others, the thief arrived and left without disturbing anything. To date, many of London's most prestigious museums have been the targets of this puzzling night-time terror. The police admit to being stumped.

How long will these attacks last? And who can stop them?

Next to the article was a small and blurry picture of the outside of a building, its window smashed, and glass scattered all over the pavement below its railings.

'Golly!' I said. 'How exciting! Someone

ought to look into it.'

'Someone certainly ought,' said Uncle Felix, scraping butter onto his toast.

'Most certainly,' agreed Aunt Lucy, sipping her tea. 'Felix dear, pass the crossword.'

By which I understood that Uncle Felix and Aunt Lucy knew far more about the thefts than they were telling us. In fact, I suspected that they were probably engaged in investigating them. I felt rather annoyed, and very jealous.

But my detective mind was at work, and it had noticed that there was something distinctly fishy about the article's picture. I looked over at Hazel to signal this to her with my eyes. But Hazel didn't look at me. She was staring at something poking out beneath the newspaper – a rather grubby-looking white envelope with some familiar writing on it.

'Alexander's written!' said Hazel, and glowed.

Alexander Arcady is a boy that Hazel and I met during the course of one of our investigations. He and his best friend, George Mukherjee, are members of the Junior Pinkertons, a rival detective society. They are not as good at solving crimes as us, but I suppose they're not bad.

But that is my opinion of Alexander, not Hazel's. I will never understand why a boy who is awkward and far too friendly and can never dress himself properly should always make Hazel look as if she has swallowed a light bulb. He only makes me feel annoyed.

'It's the Exeat this weekend, and so he's coming up to London with George. They're staying with George's parents,' said Hazel, reading through the letter and blushing furiously all the way down her neck.

I saw Uncle Felix and Aunt Lucy look up from the crossword they had begun to work on together and exchange a glance – a very married one. Then Uncle Felix said, 'I suppose they're coming to visit us?'

'No,' said Hazel, redder than ever. 'Well—'

As I have said, I think Hazel's obsession perfectly foolish. But she is my best friend, and so I said, 'Yes please, Uncle Felix.'

'Well then, write to the boys and invite them for Saturday,' said Uncle Felix, his monocle glinting as he screwed it into place over his eye. 'I shall have to think up some entertainment. You haven't had a birthday party yet, have you, Daisy?'

I ignored him. After what happened when I turned fourteen, I am quite cured of birthday parties. I am surprised that Uncle Felix isn't as well. And besides, I am fifteen years old, only five years away from twenty – far too old for birthday parties. I was more interested in what was wrong with that picture in the newspaper.

Whenever I wasn't busy with lessons that week, I drew up a list of all the museums that had been stolen from, and what had been taken. Meanwhile, Hazel spent several days practically beside herself at the thought of Alexander coming to visit, and pretending she was not. She was making a very bad job of it, as Hazel always does with her emotions.

'Come now, Hazel,' I said to her on Saturday morning, to distract her. 'Let us consider these robberies. The things the thief has stolen so far have all been jewellery and small figurines and so on. No paintings, and nothing that's difficult to carry. All the museums were attacked at night, and all were broken into with hardly any fuss. And look at the ones that have been stolen from! Practically the only one that hasn't reported a theft yet is the British Mus—'

Just then we heard a car draw up and pull away again, and then the doorbell rang. Bridget hurried to answer it. Hazel leaped up as though she had been electrified.

'I do wish you'd get over this obsession with him,' I said, scrumpling up my page of notes crossly.

'I have! I don't think of Alexander like that any more,' said Hazel thickly. 'We're only friends.'

'Rot,' I said, and pinched her in a

friendly way. 'Don't be too dreadful about it today, will you? It's bad enough that Uncle Felix keeps going on about this birthday party idea!'

Bridget came back in then, leading George and Alexander. Alexander glanced at me and turned a silly shade of red, and then looked anywhere but at me. I ignored him. George simply winked at me. I do like George.

We all said hello, and then we had that idiotic polite moment where no one is sure whether they should say what they truly want to or simply order tea. Luckily, at that point Uncle Felix poked his head round the door.

'Hello, boys,' he said. 'Nice to see you again. Do you know, I thought I'd never meet children capable of giving Daisy a run for her money, but I think the two of you – and Hazel – almost manage it. Now, I promised my niece that I would give her a birthday party.'

'*No thank you!*' I said. 'Why can't you leave it alone? I told you, I'm not a child any more!'

'Don't look at me like that!' said Uncle Felix. 'This isn't an ordinary birthday party. I know the four of you love clues and puzzles. So, how would you like to solve a mystery?'

'Yes please!' said Alexander.

My heart jumped. Could he possibly mean ... what if Uncle Felix was letting us in on what he knew about the museum thefts? I *am* fifteen now, after all. Perhaps he had finally realized that I was a brilliant detective who had solved six murder mysteries (with help from Hazel), and could be trusted.

'What's the mystery?' I asked.

'It's a treasure hunt,' said Uncle Felix. 'A series of clues that should lead you to one answer: the present I have for you. Are you game?'

I felt sick. *A treasure hunt.* I had been wrong. Uncle Felix *did* still think that I was just a child. Hazel put her hand on mine, and I realized I was clenching my fists.

'Yes please, sir,' said George politely – but I could tell that he was rather unimpressed. George is *almost* as clever as I am, and nothing but proper mysteries will do for him.

'All right,' I said, for there was nothing else to say. Uncle Felix was *dreadful*, I thought.

'I don't think you'll be disappointed,' said Uncle Felix cheerfully. 'I have the first clue all ready for you. And now for the exciting part: Lucy and I have spoken, and we have agreed that you four are to be allowed to go out on your own today, to wherever the clues take you. You are fifteen now, after all.'

He put a folded bit of paper into my hand, winked at me and ducked out of the room like a jack-in-the-box.

*

'Well!' I said. *'Well!'*

I couldn't say anything else. I was so furious that I was almost speechless, which is unusual for me.

'We're allowed out on our own!' said Hazel encouragingly. 'And perhaps the treasure hunt will be more exciting than you think?'

'You're a good person, Hazel Wong,' said George, and I knew then that he was feeling sorry for me. I was deeply ashamed of my uncle.

'Hey, it's all right,' said Alexander. 'Like Hazel says, this might be fun . . .'

I looked at last at what I had been given. It was a handwritten note in Uncle Felix's dreadful scrawl.

The world's knowledge under
Britannia's rule
visit Clio or you'll look a
fool

. _ . . / . . / _ _ _ / _ . / . . .

And on the back of it was a single letter: V.

'What dreadful doggerel,' I said, rolling my eyes. 'Really, Uncle Felix could have done better.'

'But what does it mean?' asked Alexander. 'Who's Clio? Did he spell Cleopatra wrong?'

At Deepdean I would have sighed and looked at my nails and pretended to have no idea at all, but 'out of the corner of my eye I could see that George was about to open his mouth, and no matter how much I like him, I refuse to be beaten by George Mukherjee.

'She's the Muse of History,' I said, a fraction of a second before George. 'And Britannia is the woman on all our coins, on the opposite side to the King. Her name is just a silly way of saying Britain.'

'So Britain and History,' said Alexander. 'Which means—'

'The British Museum!' I cried, once again just a fraction ahead of George, who nodded at me, grinning. 'That was easy. Honestly, Uncle Felix had better make the next clues harder. All right, I suppose we might as well get this over with. Let's go!'

I whirled out of the room to fetch our coats and hats. I do find that other people are usually so *slow*. It makes me want to grind my teeth and bite my tongue. I thrust Hazel's coat at her (the days were still blustery and fresh, and it would never do to go out in London incorrectly dressed), but she seemed half in a dream.

'Daisy,' she said, frowning. 'What about the Morse code part of the clue?'

'It hardly matters, Hazel,' I said to her. 'Come on! We already know what the clue means – we must get to the British Museum!'

*

We all four galloped out of Uncle Felix and Aunt Lucy's flat – they live in a lovely red-brick building in Bloomsbury – and rushed through the streets of London. The wind dashed after us, and pigeons scattered through the air, and a red motor car swished past and nearly blew off my hat. London moves almost as quickly as I do, and I love it. When I am grown-up, I will always live in London, and wear the very latest fashions, and there will be a brass plaque on the door of our detective agency that says: HERE LIVES THE HONOURABLE DAISY WELLS, GENIUS OF DETECTION (AND HAZEL WONG TOO).

We ran through Russell Square, the leaves on all the trees new. Up ahead was the British Museum. I made to turn left, towards Museum Street, but Hazel stopped short.

'No, not that way,' she said.

'Of course that way!' I cried. 'Britannia! She's on that triangle on the museum roof!'

'*No*,' said Hazel insistently. She really has become so bold since our Hong Kong adventure. I scarcely know what to do with her sometimes.

'Hear her out,' said Alexander. Hazel went pink and I could have stamped my foot.

'The Morse code part of the clue,' said Hazel. 'I worked it out, and it spells LIONS. Uncle Felix wants us to go round to the other entrance, where the lions are.'

The most bothersome thing about Hazel is that when she is right, she is right.

'Oh!' I said, rather wishing that I had been the one to work it out, even though I can never sit still long enough for codebreaking. 'Off we go then.'

And there, at the Montague Street entrance, flanked by two enormous lions, was Aunt Lucy.

'Bravo!' she said when she saw us. 'You cracked the first code.'

'*Hazel* cracked the code,' said George, and smiled at her.

'It was easy,' I said to Aunt Lucy, giving her a chilly glare to show that I was not to be babied.

'They do become more difficult,' said Aunt Lucy. 'Now, are you ready for your second clue?'

'Yes,' I said.

'Please,' said Hazel.

'Doesn't Hazel have lovely manners?' said Aunt Lucy. She handed Hazel another folded piece of paper. 'Felix will be waiting for you at the end of the clues, in one hour,' she said. 'Hurry along.'

We all crowded round Hazel as she unfolded the piece of paper. The clue was in Uncle Felix's handwriting again,

and was (I rolled my eyes) another one
of his dreadful poems.

> seek ye first the ancient Key
> A Frenchman was the first
> to see
> Three in one or one in three
> ...\/_\/___\/_.\/.

And on the other side we found another
bold single letter: C.

We stepped back and stared at one
another.

'Well,' said Alexander. 'Um. Are we
looking for a ... Continental lock?
Something religious? God is supposed
to be three people in one, isn't he?'

'Your god is ridiculous,' said George.
'But no, I don't think that's right. Since we're at the British Museum, it must be one of the objects.'

Hazel cleared her throat.

'What is it?' I asked.

'Well,' said Hazel, 'a *key* isn't just something that goes into a lock. It's another word for cypher – the thing that lets you break a code. And the Morse code part says STONE.'

'Oh!' said George.

'Exactly!' said Hazel.

'All right, no need to get excited, I know what it is,' I said, because I *did*. I had in fact thought of it first, and knew where we ought to go.

I led us into the museum, through the white-and-black marble entrance, up shallow marble steps and into the dusty halls of the museum itself. Lots of clever-looking grown-ups moved past us purposefully, and there was a scholarly hush to the air. I stuck my chin out, trying to look twenty, and marched through the rooms into the Egyptian sculpture gallery, making sure as I did so to keep an eye out for any suspicious clues or people.

In general, I find museums dull. I do not much care for pots and pans and small jewels. But the series of mysterious thefts had made me more interested in them – and I was also quite pleased to be in one of the Egyptian rooms. The

Egyptians are how all people from history should be, huge and fierce, and their sculptures make me feel like a queen.

'Aren't the British government ever ashamed of how much they steal?' asked George, staring around at the red and yellow and black statues. 'The British Museum has thousands more objects than it can ever display, all stored away underground, but the collectors still keep on bringing back more.'

'Shhh!' said Hazel, blushing. '*You're* British!'

'It's *not* stealing, it's finders keepers,' I said. 'Anyway, we look after them properly.'

'It's *absolutely* stealing, no matter how people look after the things they steal,' said George, raising an eyebrow. 'But I suppose we're here to inspect the Rosetta Stone, not argue.'

'Of course we are,' I said. You see, the Rosetta Stone is a huge piece of rock with three kinds of writing on it: Greek and two sorts of Egyptian. A Frenchman called Mr Champollion was the first person to realize that each bit of writing said the same thing, which meant that it could be used as a key to finally read the kind of picture writing called hieroglyphs. The stone is black and rather triangular, and sticks up like an enormous tooth in the centre of the sculpture gallery.

We all began to hunt about for the next clue. I peered at all sides of the stone, and the floor around it (a gentleman in a tweed suit said, 'Hold hard, miss!' as I pushed past him), and then began to examine the brass railing.

I was getting rather frustrated when I heard George say, 'I've got it!' I looked up and saw him peeling something from the underside of the stone's information plaque.

'No, *I've* got it!' cried Alexander a moment later. He had moved away from us and was pulling something out from between the slats of a grate at the side of the room.

Hazel and I looked from Alexander to George.

'You can't *both* have it,' I said. 'Someone must have got the wrong bit of paper.'

George frowned. 'Mine's another of those poems,' he said. 'And then there's something beneath it – I think they're hieroglyphs.'

He held up his piece of paper, and we all looked at it. It certainly matched the other two – although Uncle Felix's poem-writing had got sillier than ever.

Three for a girl, four for a boy,
Five and six for a dragon's toy.
Something to be hoarded,
something to enjoy ...

And on the other side was the letter *D*.

It did look like the next clue.

'All right, what do *you* have?' I asked Alexander.

'It isn't the same as the others at all,' he said, sounding puzzled. 'I think I must have picked up . . . a tourist's note, or something. Look!'

Beware the mummy! The old nemesis is great! Hear the awful tale, the end nigh!

And on the other side were strings of numbers:

1897,0401.95
1897,0316.1
1898,1201.20

I got a chill all up and down my spine. The hairs on my arms shivered.

'That isn't Uncle Felix's clue at all,' I said.

'It isn't,' agreed George. 'But I think it *is* a code.'

'Hey, you're right!' said Alexander. 'Just look at the first letter of each word after *Beware the mummy.*'

I looked. I have to admit that all I saw at first were words, but then I squinted and I suddenly understood.

'T – O – N – I – G – H – T – A – T – T – E – N,' I spelled out.

'Tonight at ten!' agreed George.

We all looked at each other, and I felt electric. 'We've found someone else's message,' I whispered. 'Hazel, copy it, copy it exactly! What if – *what if* this has something to do with the robberies? The papers think that they're all break-ins, but that picture I saw in the newspaper was all wrong. The glass was on the ground *outside* the museum, not on the floor inside! I think they're *inside* jobs, made to look like ordinary robberies.'

'We noticed the glass too!' said Alexander. 'That would fit!'

'If that's so, then it's not just one thief, but a group of them,' I said excitedly. 'Or the thief always has accomplices who work at the museums. What if—'

'What if the British Museum is next on the list to be robbed?' Hazel gasped. 'And this note is the thief telling his accomplice where to meet him this evening!'

'The British Museum is almost the only London museum *not* to have been attacked yet,' said George. 'It's not a bad idea, Daisy!'

'Quite true, it's a very good one,' I said. My heart was beating very fast, like a rabbit running. 'Uncle Felix may think that he's sent us to the only safe museum in London, but I think that he has in fact brought us to an extremely interesting place. We must put the message back and then follow its clue at once. Detective Society – Pinkertons – I think we have stumbled on a most important mystery!'

*

'We have to split up,' said George, as though he were in charge. Of course, I am the only one who could possibly be in charge, but George pretends not to know that.

'If we're going to investigate this note, we have to make sure we keep our cover,' he continued. 'Some of us must go on solving Uncle Felix's clues too, otherwise he'll work out what we've really been up to.'

'You can,' I said at once. 'You and Alexander.'

'I *don't* think so,' said George infuriatingly. 'One from each society, otherwise you two'll have all the fun.' It is sometimes a bother that George and I understand each other so well.

'You and Hazel, then,' I said. This was a careful calculation – I know that I am not nearly as good at breaking codes as Hazel, just as George has shown himself to be quicker at puzzles than Alexander. I also very much wanted to solve the real mystery, and did not care at all about Uncle Felix's childish treasure hunt.

'All right,' said George. 'Now, does anyone know how to read hieroglyphs?'

'I do,' said Hazel. We all looked at her. 'At least, a little. Aunt Lucy's been teaching me about them. I think I can manage to solve Uncle Felix's clue.'

This made me remember that if I'm not careful Hazel will know more than me, and that would never do.

Hazel squinted at the five hieroglyphs.

'That's a sort of K noise at the beginning,' she said. 'And an S at the end . . . and I think an N before that, and something that looks like an I?'

'Hold on, I know!' said George. 'The bit about dragons and hoarding. Dragons hoard treasure, and treasure is coins. *COINS!* And five and six are for silver and gold in that nursery rhyme, the one that begins with 'one for sorrow . . .'. We've cracked it!'

George and Hazel beamed at each other, and I thought that I had chosen very well in putting them together.

'Now, look,' said George, 'before we go off after the clues, I've got one more thing to say. I think I might know which mummy the note's talking about. You know I like unsolved mysteries?'

'Of course we do!' I said.

'All right,' said George, standing up straighter than ever. 'Listen. There's a mummy here that's called the Unlucky Mummy, because it's supposed to be *cursed*. It was first brought back from Egypt in the 1890s by four young men. Two of them *died* getting it back to England and the other two died a few months later. It was taken in by a friend of theirs, but only a few months later he brought it to the British Museum in despair. He said that it had made his daughter ill, and smashed plates in his house just like a poltergeist.'

'That's not true!' I said, seeing Hazel gulping. Hazel hates ghost stories.

'It *probably* isn't!' said George, shrugging expressively. 'It's in lots of books, though. Anyway, the next part of the story is as follows: in 1912 the British Museum tried to send it to America for an exhibition. But guess which ship they put it on?'

'The *Titanic*!' cried Alexander.

'Exactly!' said George.

'This is absolutely *not true at all*!' I protested. 'If it was, it would be at the bottom of the sea, not in the mummy room.'

'Of course that part isn't true!' said George. 'But it's a brilliant story, and lots of people believe it. They're always saying that they feel an odd presence in the mummy room. Mediums even do seances in there, to see if they can contact the Unlucky Mummy's evil spirit. It's bunkum, but there's one thing that *is* a fact: most people are afraid of the mummy room in general and the Unlucky Mummy in particular, which makes the mummy room the perfect place to hold a secret meeting – especially at night! Even the guards don't like to go in there.'

Trust George, I thought, *to somehow bring even the silliest of stories to a very sensible conclusion.*

'Very useful,' I said graciously. 'Now, will you go away to the coin room and solve the treasure hunt before we run out of time?'

'All right, all right,' said George, clapping me on the shoulder. 'Come on, Hazel, upstairs to the coin room!'

As Hazel hurried out of the Egyptian gallery with George, she looked back at Alexander and blushed. It really does infuriate me that, around Alexander, Hazel turns back into the shy little girl I first met at Deepdean years ago, and not the downright fearsome detective she has become. He is no good for her *at all*. He really isn't, Hazel. I'm only saying it in your best interests.

'All right,' I said, standing like the leader of the group, which I was, then turned to Alexander. 'The important thing now is to uncover more about this clue. Come on, Wats— Alexander.' (For there is only one person in the world who is worthy of that nickname.) 'We must go and investigate this cursed mummy. And, while we do, we must also come up with a list of suspects. It's clear that the person who left the note could be any member of staff or visitor – but who could they leave it *for*? Who might be able to get into the museum at ten o'clock at night, after it's closed?'

'A visitor might hide until after closing,' offered Alexander, brushing the sandy hair back from his forehead. 'But I guess that's unlikely. OK, how about one of the museum staff? A keeper, or a guard.'

'A guard isn't a bad idea,' I said grudgingly. 'Someone who wouldn't look odd wandering around after dark. Now, where are these mummies?'

I had to admit that, even though I don't believe in ghosts, the mummy room was eerie. Cases loomed at us out of the dimness, menacingly still, and all the wrinkly professors and hungry-looking students and tired nannies dragging little children about the gallery seemed unusually subdued.

Alexander was rushing around, disturbing the dust and all the other visitors as he peered excitedly at the labels next to the mummy cases.

I tried to look as though I didn't

know who he was, but he rather ruined this by shouting, 'Hey, Daisy, it's this one!' and waving his arm at me in its too-short shirtsleeve.

'Shush!' I said. 'You'll make people suspicious!'

'Not me,' said Alexander, grinning infuriatingly. 'I'm just an American kid who likes mummies. What's suspicious about that? Come and look! It's spooky.'

As I said, I don't believe in ghosts. That is all Hazel. But ... looking up into the fixed, flat-eyed glare of the Unlucky Mummy made the back of my neck feel distinctly uncomfortable. Her face was very blank and calm, and her hands were crossed over her patterned and painted breast. There were winged figures all down her body, and they looked unpleasant.

'Just think!' said Alexander. 'This case used to hold a *real* dead body.'

'And this room is full of them!' I said. 'I wonder if any of them were murdered.'

Then I scowled, because I had caught myself agreeing with Alexander about something, and that would never do.

'We must search this room for further clues,' I announced. 'We have to solve the mystery of those strings of numbers, after all.'

'I thought they might be locations,' said Alexander. 'You know, latitudes and longitudes. But they don't look quite right.'

I refuse to say it to him, but perhaps

Alexander is not the *worst* detective in the world. I was very glad, though, when it was me who solved the mystery of the numbers.

I was peering into a small case loaded with jewellery. At first my eyes were dazzled by the bright gold rings and chains, but then I looked at the scraps of paper next to each one. Each label had a description and two numbers, a short one and a longer one – and they exactly matched the pattern of our numbers.

'Oh!' I said. 'Alexander, come here!'

Once we'd made that breakthrough, it was not hard to discover what the numbers belonged to. The first was next to a thick gold signet ring; the second was next to a slender gold and garnet necklace; and the last was next to a grey scarab beetle, engraved with the image of a hawk.

'So, what does it mean?' asked Alexander.

'Well, *obviously*,' I said, not exactly knowing what I was going to say next, 'obviously . . . they're . . .' And then I knew. 'It's a list!' I cried. 'A shopping list, like Bridget or our housekeeper Mrs Doherty would make, only disguised. They're the things the thief has asked for from his contact here.'

'Of course!' said Alexander enthusiastically. 'That must be it! But – hey, they're only little things, just like the ones stolen from the other museums. Don't you think that's weird?

I mean, if you were breaking into the British Museum, wouldn't you steal more important objects?'

'I expect they're extremely valuable,' I said – but really I had to admit that Alexander was right. They did seem awfully little things to break into a museum for. Was there more to this mystery than we had yet deduced?

Hazel and George came running in then, breathless and very pleased with themselves.

'We solved them all!' said Hazel triumphantly.

'Hazel solved most of them,' said George. 'I just watched.'

'Coin room, then chessmen, then Elgin Marbles, then Assyrian lions,' said

Hazel, ticking them off on her fingers. 'And the letters: V, C, D, Q, I, O. They must spell out something, but we don't know what yet.'

I blinked. 'I know what they mean,' I said, and I got a funny twinge, because perhaps I shouldn't have been so rude about Uncle Felix's birthday present. 'Now, where is Uncle Felix waiting for us?'

'There you are!' I said, marching over with the other three behind me.

Uncle Felix turned in mock surprise from where he was posing next to one of the statues in the Greek room, his long, smooth face fitting in perfectly with the senator he was in front of.

'Not bad,' he said, screwing in his monocle and looking down at me (less far down than he used to – I have grown so much that now I nearly reach his shoulder). 'Forty-five minutes to solve the clues. Now, I have a present for you. I assume you know what it is?'

'Vidocq,' I said, scowling as hard as I could so as not to show how pleased I was. 'The French policeman who invented being a detective. You can't have bought me him, since he's dead and it's not polite to buy people anyway, so I suppose you've got me the book he wrote.'

'The first English edition,' said Uncle Felix. 'I thought it was fitting for my detective niece. Here you are.'

I do not hug Uncle Felix often – he is not a hugging sort of person, and neither am I – but I hugged him then.

'Now, I thought the four of you might like to go and have some tea,' said Uncle Felix. 'I have to— Well, something has come up at work.'

'Oh, is it the museum thief?' asked Alexander eagerly. George poked him, but it was too late.

'None of your business,' said Uncle Felix firmly, taking a step back and glaring at us. 'Do you want tea or not?'

Suddenly I found myself feeling cross with him all over again. It was not fair that Uncle Felix should call me a detective with one breath and then tell me I wasn't old enough to detect with the next. If I had been unsure about discussing the message we had found with Uncle Felix, or about following the clue ourselves, I wasn't any more.

I looked around the Greek gallery – at the old lady wrapped up in a great grey scarf, the little boy pointing at all the rude bits of the statues while his nanny tried to drag him away, and the guard standing to attention beside the door. None of them *seemed* very suspicious, but I have learned that you cannot count on people's appearances at all. Was the thief's accomplice hiding in plain sight?

'Here,' said Uncle Felix, holding out his hand and interrupting my thoughts. 'For your tea.' It was a ten-shilling note.

'Thank you, Uncle,' I said coolly, taking the note between my fingers as though it were a dead mouse. 'We shall go and get some ices.'

'Uncle Felix is treating us like children!' I said bitterly as we walked out of the museum, past a cleaning woman mopping the floor, then a tweedy lady making notes in a book, and finally past a policeman pacing to and fro on the steps. When I saw him, I knew that the police *must* be worried about a break-in here soon.

'We *are* children,' said George. 'Technically, at least.'

'We are *detectives*!' I said. 'And I know that he's been working on this mystery.

It's simply not fair of him to keep us in the dark. It'll serve him right if we are the ones who solve it. Oh, come on, I'll tell you my plan over tea.'

There was an old woman feeding the pigeons on the museum steps, her hair down around her shoulders. Alexander gave her tuppence, and Hazel glowed up at him most infuriatingly.

'Really, why does everyone have to be obsessed with *love*? It's a dreadful distraction,' I muttered to George while the other two walked ahead.

'I look forward to you falling in love,' said George. 'I only hope I shall be there to see it.'

'*I never shall*,' I said, and I meant it then. Love is a silly emotion, and does not help a detective do their job. I know that Hazel sometimes has wondered whether I am in love with George, but of course she is quite wrong. He's all right as far as boys go, very tall and clean, but I have discovered that when I look at boys I cannot see what Hazel does.

'So, what are we going to do?' asked Alexander once we were all sitting around the tea-room table with our ices in front of us. The sun was shining outside, and in any other circumstances it would have been a lovely birthday treat. But I was so excited and upset that I could hardly eat mine, although I knew this went quite against the

Detective Society rule of never saying no to tea.

'We're going to break into the British Museum this evening and discover who the thief is,' I said. 'What else could we possibly do?'

'It's awfully dangerous, though!' said Hazel.

'The only things worth doing are dangerous ones, Hazel. Don't you know that by now?' I asked. Anyone would think that Hazel was new to the Detective Society.

Hazel blushed and said, 'I don't mean we shouldn't do it! Only – we ought to be sure it's worth it.'

'Of course it is, and of course we should do it,' said George. 'It's a brilliant adventure, and Alex and I haven't had many of those lately. Alex, what do you say?'

'Daisy's right,' said Alexander. 'And – look, we don't have to actually surprise the thief, do we? Just watch and find out who he is. So it's not *really* dangerous. We can tell the police once we know his identity.'

'And the identity of the person in the British Museum helping him,' agreed Hazel. 'A keeper could unlock the displays, and a guard would have keys and a reason to be about late at night. It must be one of them – it has to be an inside job!'

'Quite right,' I said.

'Detectives, I've had an idea,' said George, eyes widening. 'I know where we can hide for the meeting – somewhere we'll never be discovered.'

'No,' said Hazel, very forcefully for her. 'No! I know what you're going to say, and – absolutely not!'

'Where?' I asked suspiciously.

'Inside the mummy cases,' said Hazel. 'That's what you were going to say, isn't it, George?'

It was an absolutely brilliant idea, and I was furious that I hadn't thought of it first.

'But they've got bodies in them!' cried Alexander, looking disgusted and delighted all at once.

'Hazel's quite right. And no, most of them haven't any more,' said George. 'Grave robbers took them out years before they ever arrived in London. If we get into the cases, no one will notice we're there!'

'This is the most horrid idea I have ever heard,' I said. 'We absolutely *must* do it. Well *done*, George!'

Hazel looked rather ill, and so did Alexander. They are both much too tender-hearted. But George's eyes were sparkling, and I could feel myself beaming back at him. 'All right,' I said. 'Now, how do we go about breaking into the museum?'

'There must be floorplans in the

Reading Room,' said George. 'You girls go home—'

'You are *not* to have adventures without us!' I cried. 'This is *our* mystery!'

'You girls go home,' continued George, 'and see if you can have a look at your uncle's files.' He raised his eyebrows at me. 'You think he's been working on the case. Well then, see if he's found out anything that might be useful to us. *We'll* look at the plans. Then we'll go back to my house, pretend to go to bed as normal and meet you at nine p.m. at the edge of Russell Square.'

'Oh,' I said. 'I suppose that isn't a *bad* idea.'

In fact, I could feel myself becoming enthusiastic. This sounded like a proper spy mission.

'All right,' said George, nodding. 'Now, go home and pretend to be ordinary.'

'I am never ordinary,' I said, drawing myself up to my full height. 'But I shall be ordinarily brilliant.'

The rest of that day was dreadfully dull, but at the same time rather lovely, like Christmas Eve, when you know you have really splendid presents waiting for you the next morning.

Hazel distracted Bridget by asking her to make tea, and then we quickly rifled through Uncle Felix's desk, in case he had left any interesting information about the case. We didn't find much — but there was enough to show that he definitely was investigating. I found an official-looking letter that read:

Dear M: London black market flooded with valuable artefacts. Most can be matched to those reported stolen, but there are additional items of such fine quality that they must come from another museum collection, perhaps several. Are the thieves able to steal without raising the alarm? Are we dealing with a larger gang than we assumed? Please investigate. Check persons of interest at the museums - we cannot rule out guards and curators as suspects.

And there was one other thing: a scribbled note that said:

> You'll never get your things back.
> Give up now!!

It seemed to have been marked up by a handwriting expert: *Over-confident Y. Aggressive G. Clearly male.* There was also a note in Uncle Felix's writing that said:

> An unpleasant adversary. This man will attempt the next robbery soon.

'Look!' said Hazel. 'That first note – the writing matches the one we found!'

She took her bit of paper with the copy of the message we had discovered in the British Museum out of her pocket and put it next to the one on Uncle Felix's desk. 'See?'

It did indeed, and I felt jumpy all over with excitement. We really were on the right track. I remembered what Alexander had said – that it was odd to break into the British Museum for such small objects. Perhaps that was the key to solving this mystery. Had the thief been using his contact inside the museum to steal smaller items without anyone noticing? But – why *had* no one noticed things missing from their cases?

Then Bridget called that the tea was ready, and we had to hurry away.

After dinner was cleared, Hazel and I went into our room and pretended to be getting ready for bed. Really, of course, we were changing out of our day things into the dark tunics and trousers that Hazel had brought back for us from Hong Kong. Her maid, Ping, had tried to alter mine to fit me, and it almost works, although it's still short in the arms and legs.

We took out our pyjamas, wrapped them around the bolsters from our beds, and then hid them in the wardrobe, to be used later to imitate our sleeping forms in case anyone looked into our room while we were gone. We were lying down under our covers perfectly sweetly when Aunt Lucy came in to turn out the lights.

'Goodnight, girls,' she said as she closed the door. 'Well done on your detecting today.'

I knew that Hazel would be feeling rather guilty at that.

'Quick,' I said as soon as Aunt Lucy's footsteps had died away. 'Put your bolster in your bed and let's go!'

We climbed out of the bedroom window and balanced on the low balcony that runs round the building. The flats are usefully corniced and pillared, and it really was easy work to creep down the side. Of course, Hazel made heavy weather of it – but in the end we both managed it with not much more than scraped knees.

We were lucky. A lovely yellowish London fog was curling around us, smothering the street lights and muffling our breath and our footsteps. It was cold and soft where it touched my skin, just like walking through velvet.

We hared off, and it was a good thing that I had set myself to memorize London's streets, for the fog made everything strange. Once a blue-coated policeman came swinging by, and I had to pull Hazel into the shelter of an archway so he would not see us. Nice little girls do not go out at night. It was rather exhilarating to be free of being nice and little for a while.

Then the black railings of Russell Square Gardens loomed up in front of us. We followed them round until we turned a corner and heard a voice say, 'Hello? Who goes there?'

'It's us, you chump,' I said, for I recognized Alexander's voice at once. A moment later, he appeared. 'And it's no good asking *Who goes there*? What would you have done if it had been someone else?'

'We can look after ourselves,' said George, his figure swimming out of the fog to stand next to us. 'We're tall, dark strangers, after all.'

'You're boys in unsuitable clothes,' I said, for both he and Alexander were wearing their light spring coats and hats. I could see Alexander shivering. 'Now, shall we get on? Have you discovered how to break into the British Museum?'

'Of course we have,' said George. 'There's a gate on Montague Street. You'll see.'

'And what if we run into a guard?' I asked.

'We thought of that,' said George coolly. 'We came early so we could hang about outside the gate. There's a guard station just inside it – we can hear someone doing their rounds. Footsteps arrive and go away again every twenty minutes, but there's no talking, and no sound of dogs. We think he's alone.'

'Very good,' I said reluctantly. 'And once we're inside?'

'There's an easy route,' said George. 'Alex has it mapped out.'

'The place is huge!' said Alexander. 'I had no idea it was so big. There really are gigantic storerooms in the cellar for all the objects they can't show upstairs. All those treasures, and nobody ever sees them! There are offices too, but I've worked out a way for us to the passage that leads up to the mummy room without going past very many of them. If we're caught—'

'If we're caught, we're the nieces and nephews of some of the keepers, and their friends,' I said. 'Now, lead on to the gate.'

When we got to the Montague Street gate, I stopped short.

'You didn't research this properly!' I cried. 'This isn't a gate! It's a door!'

It was true. The gate was tall and black, and set snugly into the side of the museum. There was no way over it, not if you were any bigger than a mouse.

'It's quite all right,' said George calmly. 'If you get up onto the top of that wall to our left, there, we'll show you how we can get in.'

The house to the left of the museum had white pillars on each side of its door, and a tall brick wall to its right. By shinning up the pillars and stretching, we managed to reach the top of the wall. (Hazel had to be pushed a little by George.) I crouched low and peered into the darkness.

'*There*,' whispered George. 'Look ahead. The museum may have a secure gate, but the back garden of this house shares a wall with it, and we can get over that. Beyond the wall is an alleyway, and on the other side of the alley is the museum itself. There's a door that opens straight into it. I told you it was all right. We should have ten minutes before the guard comes back here. Come on!'

Along the wall we moved, treading as carefully as cats over loose and missing bricks, and when we came to the end, we jumped down onto a little tarmacked path. In front of us was the great side of the museum – and in that side was a small door.

'Here,' whispered Alexander. 'See?'

While the others waited, I took a pin out of my hair to pick the lock (I've had practice). But it transpired that I didn't need to – the door swung open under my hand.

'Oh!' whispered Alexander. 'Of course – the accomplice! The door must have been left open for the thief!'

The idea that the thief might be on his way gave me the most wonderful thrill of excitement, but I saw Hazel start with horror. I patted her comfortingly, and pushed her through.

I followed – and there we were, inside the British Museum. In front of us was a long, shadowed corridor. Pipes trailed overhead, boxes were piled all the way down it and there was a smell in the air of very old dust.

'It *smells* like a mummy,' whispered Hazel.

'How do you know what a mummy smells like?' I asked her. But, as we crept along, stepping round boxes and crates, I privately agreed.

At the end of the corridor we turned right, then right again, and found ourselves at the bottom of a set of stairs.

Up those we went, and came out onto the museum's ground floor.

'Hey! There's a guard!' hissed George, and we all flattened ourselves against an overhanging wall while footsteps swung past, and cheerful whistling grew loud in our ears and then faint again.

It was all the best fun, and made my heart race excitingly in my chest. I don't know how anyone can bear to be ordinary, and live a dull life, when they could be creeping through dark buildings at night on crucial secret missions.

I was quite giddy by the time we slipped into the mummy gallery, although I could tell that Hazel was having Rather a bad time of it. She kept giving little shudders and drawing close to me. I patted her on the arm to tell her to buck up, and she nodded back at me, her face set.

Alexander whispered, 'Creepy!'

'Shh!' George and I both said at once.

It was true that the room was more eerie than ever now that the museum was dark and silent. The mummies loomed all around us, their painted faces just visible and looking extremely stern. I almost thought that I saw one breathing – but of course that was the most Hazel-ish nonsense. I told myself not to be silly.

'Where do we hide?' asked Alexander.

George pointed. 'I know that one's empty, and that one, and that one – and, of course, the Unlucky Mummy too.'

Hazel let out a very small noise.

'Oh, for heaven's sake, I'll take that one,' I said. 'There isn't any curse, Hazel. You know that!'

But, as I slipped behind the mummy's bird-painted front into the empty space behind it, I got a most unaccustomed feeling – of dread.

Perhaps it was because it was so unpleasantly easy to do, or perhaps it was because it moved just a little as I did so, making a soft little creak that somehow sounded rather like a small scream.

But I gritted my teeth and ignored the noise. I knew it was no good giving in to silliness. Good detectives never allow themselves to become so het up that they cannot properly observe the scene. I peeped round into the gallery, reminding myself to breathe slowly and calmly. I saw Hazel climbing into her case with a most imploring look in my direction, and George slipping into his with delight all over his face.

The mummy gallery was absolutely silent. And then—

'Daisy,' said Hazel very clearly.

'Shhhh!' we all said.

'Daisy, I don't have the message. It's not in my pocket. I think I left it on Uncle Felix's desk. DAISY!'

'Not now! Quiet!' I hissed urgently. 'Someone's coming!'

And they were. My heart hammered like a rabbit caught in a trap as the footsteps approached, and someone walked into the gallery.

I looked – and for a moment I thought there had been some kind of mistake. The person who had appeared was short and very stout, wearing a pinny and a kerchief, and wheeling a mop and bucket. She was, unmistakably, a cleaning woman. I had a vision of jumping out to warn her of the peril she was in, at the probable expense of my own life (I would make a lovely corpse, and it would be for a noble cause), but I paused, and then was glad I did.

A minute later, another woman came in after her. She was thinner and taller, wearing dark clothing and carrying a rucksack on her back. She looked every inch a thief. And I wondered why on earth we had all been so sure that the person behind so many robberies was a man.

'Evening,' said the plump cleaning woman calmly. 'How are you, my love?'

'Very well, Beryl,' said the thin woman. 'Now, do you have the objects I asked for?'

The cleaning woman reached into her bucket and pulled out a bundle wrapped in newspaper. 'Here you are – all three – though I couldn't quite match the ring. I found something near enough, I hope. Take a look.'

The thin woman made a small annoyed noise. 'Humph!' she said. 'Well, I suppose you tried. Now, hand them over, and I'll give you your payment.'

The case fell into place in my head. I thought of Bridget, and the way she can be clever without anyone noticing. I thought of how the list of objects had reminded me of one of Mrs Doherty's shopping lists. We had suspected a keeper or a guard, but of course cleaners knew the museum too, and its objects. A cleaning woman could be here at night, and leave a door open for the thief – the *female* thief. Girls can be detectives, just as much as boys. So why shouldn't a girl become a master criminal?

I remembered what George and Alexander had said too: that there were huge rooms below the museum, full of objects that the galleries couldn't display. What if the requests were not for the objects in the cases, but for objects *like* them from those packed away downstairs? *They* would never be missed.

I knew I had the answer. But something else was happening. Beryl, the cleaning woman, had brought in an air of dust around her, and it added to the dust of the room and the corridors. And, although I am usually perfectly in control of myself, in this particular instance my nose acted independently of me in the most traitorous way.

I hardly like to write it, but the fact is that at that moment – I sneezed.

It was a very loud sneeze, and it echoed about the room, and Beryl yelled and dropped the packet she was holding out. It fell to the floor, clinking, and out of it rolled a golden ring and a little stone scarab, and something else that I didn't have the chance to see before the black-clad woman rushed across the room and pulled me out from behind the mummy case – which was turning out to be very unlucky indeed.

I kicked out with all my might, and she yelled but did not drop me.

Then I heard several voices at once.

'Put her DOWN!' screamed Hazel, shoving her mummy case open with a bang.

'Drop her! Drop her!' shouted George and Alexander, leaping out of theirs.

'You little rats!' screamed the criminal mastermind, and she took me by the neck and shook me so hard and so ferociously that her face blurred in front of me. My throat was hurting dreadfully, and I was furious with her, and with myself. I clawed at her cheeks. She yelled, and shook me even harder, and then there was a very loud noise, and all at once I was falling to the floor and the woman's hands were no longer around my neck.

Although my mind is brilliant, I had been quite shaken by my adventure, and so it took me a moment to realize that the loud noise had been someone shouting. It took me another moment to make sure that I had not been hurt – and then I sat up quickly, my neck aching like anything, and looked about.

The two women were crouching on the floor with their hands up. Hazel, looking extremely warlike, was standing between me and them, and behind her was Uncle Felix and a whole group of very menacing-looking policemen.

'Uncle Felix!' I croaked.

'Daisy!' gasped Hazel. 'You're all right!' She knelt down and threw her arms about me. That hurt.

'Do stop it,' I said, through my very sore throat. 'Haven't I told you that heroines never die?'

'Daisy Wells,' said Uncle Felix in his coldest voice, 'you are in more trouble than you can possibly imagine. Now, the police will be taking these two women outside to their Black Maria, and I will be helping them, and while I do so the four of you will follow me in absolute silence. Do you understand?'

'Yes, Uncle Felix,' I said. 'But, if you *do* need help, you should tell us.'

'George and I can tie excellent knots . . . began Alexander – and withered under Uncle Felix's glare.

The four of us followed Uncle Felix and the policemen as they led the two women out of the museum in handcuffs. We were in the most terrible trouble, some of the worst we had ever been in, but—

'We *did* catch the thieves,' I whispered.

'And how!' George whispered back. 'Pinkertons and Detective Society for ever!'

We all beamed at each other, very secretly.

When we got back to the flat, Uncle Felix's wrath was terrible. I was almost impressed. He shouted at us for quite ten minutes about being impertinent idiots who thought we were detectives.

'We *are* detectives!' I said, again and again. 'We caught the criminals, and I wouldn't really have died – anyway, *you* were there. We left the incriminating note for you on purpose.'

We had not, but Uncle Felix did not need to know that.

'Doesn't it prove that we are good at solving crime?' I asked.

'YOU ALMOST GOT YOURSELVES KILLED!' bellowed Uncle Felix.

'And *you* almost got yourself killed twice last month,' said Aunt Lucy, who was watching the argument from a chair in the living room. 'Felix dear, do calm down. You've caught the thief you were looking for, and it *was* an inside job, just as you thought. That woman had worked at a whole string of museums under various different aliases, and I suppose she recruited her accomplices from her old friends. A gang of criminal charwomen, how clever!'

Uncle Felix sighed hugely. 'Well,' he said, 'I suppose I did. And it was clever of you.'

'It was!' I cried.

'BUT,' he went on, 'you must stop putting yourself in danger. You know I have to at least *appear* to look after you, tiresome child.'

'We *both* do,' said Aunt Lucy. 'Now, Felix, do let the children explain their side of the story. I'm dying to know. Bridget has called George's father, and he should be here in half an hour. I shall look after Daisy's injuries while they tell us all about it.'

Aunt Lucy smeared arnica on my bruises, and we told her how the treasure hunt had led us to uncover a real criminal plot. It sounded even more thrilling now that it was over.

'I must say,' Uncle Felix said rather grudgingly when we had finished, 'one day you might be rather good spies.'

'We're good spies *now*!' I said. 'In fact, we're quite brilliant.'

'Indeed,' he said drily. 'All the same, I would prefer you to work up to it more slowly. Boys, you will be safely back at school by Monday, but – let's see – we need to find something to occupy Hazel and Daisy; something not remotely criminal. It's a good thing you'll be with them, Lucy. Make sure they're bored this week, will you?'

I rolled my eyes. Aunt Lucy smiled.

But that is really the funniest part of this whole story. Because our utterly boring week . . . turned out to be not so boring after all. In fact, it turned out to lead us straight to the Rue Theatre.

Hazel's Guide to the British Museum

I've read through Daisy's account of our case. There are some words that I think might be confusing for readers who do not know England as well as Daisy does, and so I have created this guide. Daisy says it is not necessary, but Daisy does not know everything (Yes I do! – Daisy), and so I have done it anyway.

- **Alias** – a word for a false name used by someone to hide their identity.

- **Arnica** – a plant that can be turned into a cream to help with cuts and bruises.
- **Artefact** – a precious, ancient object in a museum.
- **Black Maria** – a police van that takes criminals to prison.
- **Bolster** – a long thick roll-shaped pillow that goes behind the other pillows on a bed. If you stuff it down the length of a bed, not across it, you can make it look as though someone is still sleeping in the bed.
- **Bunkum** – a word meaning nonsense.
- **Charwoman** – another word for a cleaning woman.
- **Chump** – one of Daisy's favourite words, which means idiot.
- **Curator** – someone who looks after objects in a museum.

- **Doggerel** – poetry or verse that is badly written, sometimes on purpose.
- **Exeat** – a long weekend when schoolchildren are allowed to leave their school and go visit family or friends.
- **Keeper** – a special British Museum word for curator.
- **Latitude** – imaginary lines around the globe showing how far north or south a place is from the Equator.
- **Longitude** – imaginary lines around the globe showing how far east or west a place is from the Meridian line in Greenwich, London.
- **Monocle** – a sort of round eyeglass that you squeeze into place over one eye.
- **Pinny** – an apron.
- **Reading Room** – a place in the British Museum where scholars can sit and read any

book that has ever been published in England.
It sounds like heaven.

- **Shilling** — twelve pence. There are twenty
  shillings in a pound.

Author's Note And Acknowledgements

When I was a child, my mother worked at the Ashmolean Museum in Oxford. I learned plenty of odd things, including the hieroglyphic alphabet, what ought to go into canopic jars and the different glazes on Greek pottery. The hieroglyphics in this book are based on the ones I used to write messages to my friends – but of course the hieroglyphic alphabet does not really map onto the modern

Western alphabet. Any list of letters is a bit of a fudge, so apologies if what I have written does not tally with what you know. There are hundreds of slightly different interpretations! Thank you to my mother, Kathie Booth Stevens, for raising me among Egyptian tombs and ram statues, and for making sure that the hieroglyphic alphabet in this story is as correct as it can be for these purposes.

When I was in my early twenties, I spent six months working at the British Museum Press on Montague Street, my very first job in publishing. Walking through the British Museum every day was an incredible experience, and that time also greatly inspired this story. I want to thank Alice, Claudia, Kate, Amanda and the rest of the British Museum Press team for giving me such a wonderful experience, and for being so kind and helpful.

Although museums in England obviously mean a lot to me, I know that it isn't really possible to discuss the beauty of the objects in them without acknowledging the often painful history of their acquisition. British explorers and archaeologists generally took the untroubled view that the world was theirs for the taking, and they swept up artefacts with little thought for the rights of the people who lived near the sites they were excavating. There are now movements in many countries to get back the pieces of their history that the British took, and arguments as to whether objects belong in a British museum or in the country they were found have raged for a very long time. It is hard to be absolute about something so complicated, but in general I am on George's side.

The Unlucky Mummy is absolutely real, and still on display at the British Museum, though the mummy room has moved from its place in the 1930s. However, if you do go to visit, I would ask you to NOT try and touch any of the objects, or climb into any mummy cases. In real life, this is frowned upon.

As always, I would like to thank my agent, Gemma Cooper, my team at Puffin (Naomi Colthurst, Natalie Doherty, Tom Rawlinson, Harriet Venn, Sonia Razvi, Ellen Grady, Louise Dickie, Stephanie Barrett, Jane Tait, Dominica Clements), my cover illustrator, Nina Tara, and my husband, David Stevens. And thanks to my friend Anne Miller for the read-through!

And finally, thanks to Waterstones and to booksellers across the country for their years of incredible support. I feel so lucky that you have all embraced Daisy and Hazel so enthusiastically – I owe this story to you.

HIEROGLYPHIC ALPHABET

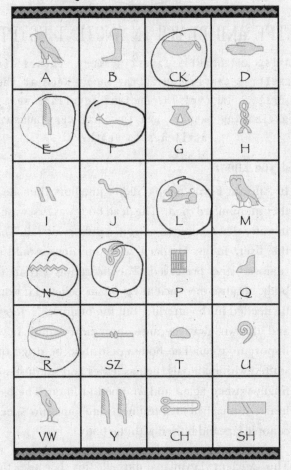

If you're interested in Morse Code, a key can be found
in our other case book CREAM BUNS AND CRIME

LIFE AND DEATH IN ANCIENT EGYPT!

Daisy and Hazel's latest mystery reaches its exciting conclusion in the Mummy Room at the British Museum! The Ancient Egyptians were fascinating people, and they had very unusual attitudes to death.

Did you know:

- In Ancient Egypt, people didn't just bury their dead, they mummified them! The dead body was first washed in water that contained natron, a preserving salt. Then the liver, lungs, stomach and intestines would be removed and preserved. The heart was left in the body, because the Ancient Egyptians believed it would be needed in the afterlife. But the brain was removed and thrown away, because they didn't think it was important at all! The body would then be dried out, stuffed with materials such as leaves and sawdust, and finally washed again and wrapped in linen. The liver, lungs, stomach and intestines were put into special canopic jars and buried with the body.

- The Ancient Egyptians did all this because they believed that the afterlife was a very important

place, and that the spirits of the dead would go on a journey there. They thought that once this journey was completed, a person could continue to live a happy and easy life, as long as they made sure they had the proper supplies and possessions with them in their grave. Rich people would have little clay models of their houses, their favourite pieces of furniture and even their servants made, so that when they arrived in the next world they would be able to have the same lifestyle as they had enjoyed in this one!

- But the journey of the dead wasn't an easy one. There were many trials to overcome and monsters to fight, and spirits needed all the help they could get. Osiris – the god of the afterlife – was painted on the linen shroud and on the outside of the coffin. Amulets (good luck charms) were also wrapped in the linen to protect the body throughout its journey into the underworld.

- To be absolutely sure that a spirit stayed safe, though, they needed one more thing: the help of a spell-book, the Book of the Dead. The Book of the Dead

would be the spirit's guide through a series of gates and to the Hall of Judgement, where the jackal-headed god Anubis would weigh your heart on a set of scales. If you had behaved well in life, your heart would be lighter than a feather and you could go on to your promised happy afterlife. But if you had been a bad person, the scales would tip and your heart would be eaten by the Devourer, a terrible beast with a crocodile head, a lion body and the hind legs of a hippo.

- The Pharaohs, the kings of Ancient Egypt, were mummified in great style and often buried within pyramids. These rulers were incredibly powerful and rich. A Pharaoh was usually a man, but not always! At least six women have ruled as Pharaoh, including Cleopatra, Sobekneferu and Hatshepsut. You can't be sure of the gender of a pharaoh just from looking at paintings and sculptures of them – often, female Pharaohs wore false wooden beards, just like male Pharaohs, to show their importance.

- Perhaps the most famous Pharaoh was Tutankhamun. Tutankhamun was just nine years old when he took the throne from his father, Akhenaten, an unusual Pharaoh

who tried to ban all gods apart from the sun god, Aten. Tutankhamun was also very young when he died – analysis of his mummy suggests he was only eighteen or nineteen. Was his death an accident? Was he ill? Or was there foul play at work? Tutankhamun's tomb was discovered in 1922 by Howard Carter, a British Egyptologist. It was an incredibly rich find – unusually, it had not been plundered by grave robbers, and all its fabulous gold and jewels were still present. But legend has it that there was a curse on anyone who found the tomb, and certainly the discovery was followed by tragedy. Several of the people who were with Carter during his excavation of the tomb died mysteriously afterwards – including one from an infected mosquito bite, one from a fever he developed after visiting the tomb, and one from arsenic poisoning. It could just be a coincidence . . . or a case that only the Detective Society and the Junior Pinkertons could crack . . .

WRITE LIKE AN EGYPTIAN!

Find out more about the ancient alphabet:

- The word *hieroglyphs* is Greek – even though the alphabet is Egyptian! *Hiero* means 'holy' and *glyph* means 'mark' or 'writing', so the word means 'holy writing'. It's the writing used by Pharaohs and priests, and it can be found carved into stone or painted onto walls at temples and in pyramids and tombs.

- The Ancient Egyptians couldn't write on the kind of paper we know today – it hadn't been invented! Instead they used *papyrus*, a kind of paper made from plants called reeds, which were dried in the sun, flattened and stuck together.

- If Ancient Egyptians wanted to write down a contract or a shopping list, they wouldn't have used hieroglyphic writing to do it. Instead, scribes used *hieratic* – a simplified form of hieroglyphs that's easier to write. (Imagine it as a little like the shorthand Hazel and Alexander use!) Hieratic was eventually simplified even more into a new form of writing called *demotic*. But it's thought that fewer than ten in every hundred Egyptians could actually read or write.

- The Rosetta Stone, which Daisy and Hazel visit, contains the same text written in hieroglyphic, demotic and Greek. It's still in the British Museum today – so you can go and see it for yourself!

CODEBREAKERS!

Can you crack these codes like Hazel and George?
Use the hieroglyphic alphabet on p.103 to help!

1. ⟨hieroglyphs⟩ C U R S E D

c u r s e d

Clue: According to the mysterious story George tells the Detective Society, you should stay away from one of the mummies in the British Museum because it might be . . .

2. ⟨hieroglyphs⟩ M U S E U M

Clue: Newspapers have been reporting break-ins to places like this all across London.

3. ⟨hieroglyphs⟩

M _ _ S _ _ _ _ _ _

Clue: One day, Hazel and Daisy will own the world's finest consulting detective agency so they can solve plenty of these.

4. ⟨hieroglyphs⟩ _ _ _ _ _ _

Clue: The people who are supposed to make sure that no one steals from museums!

Turn over to read an extract from Daisy and Hazel's next thrilling mystery:

DEATH IN THE SPOTLIGHT

1

My name is Hazel Wong, and I am a detective.

When Daisy and I first began investigating mysteries, it simply didn't seem possible that someone like me *could* detect. But now I cannot imagine my life without Daisy Wells and the Detective Society, without strange events and awful danger and horrid heart-pounding surprises. There is always a moment, when we are deep in the midst of a case, when I think that I never want to detect another after that one is done. But all the same, if more than a few months go by without a murder, or a theft, or a kidnapping, I begin to feel as though something is missing.

Even by Detective Society standards, though, we are having a most exciting few weeks. We are proper members of a real London theatre company, and thus closer to being grown-up than ever before – and as well as that, we have once again found ourselves faced with a ghastly and shocking crime. I truly do feel almost like one of the heroines of Daisy's mystery novels.

Of course, a book heroine would not have a spot on her nose, she would not be so fond of cakes (I do not mind about this difference, for in my opinion many heroines do not eat nearly enough), and she would have no trouble remembering her lines in a play. I have fallen short of all three of those things, and even Daisy, with her clear skin and her excellent acting, loves cake. So it is clear that we are real, and really facing our *seventh* murder case. I remember a time when I was surprised we had even got to three.

I ought to explain exactly how we got *here*, sitting in the dusty, greasepaint-smelling stalls of the Rue Theatre, while a large, blue-hatted policeman tromps about on stage and shouts at us all to *sit tight and not go anywhere.*

Of course, the policeman is here today, and so are we, because of the corpse – which is not a pleasant thing to have to write. Dead bodies are always awful. They are my least favourite part of what Daisy and I do. Daisy is sometimes impatient with me when I say this. But all the same, I am glad they upset me. I do not think I would be as good a detective if I stopped caring about the victims. Murder *matters*, and bothering about it helps us solve each case.

But this mystery properly began a few weeks ago, with Daisy's Aunt Lucy and Uncle Felix. They are the reason that we are at the Rue, and it is funny to think that we were sent here to keep us *out* of detective trouble.

'Ooh,' Daisy has just hissed under her breath from the seat next to me. 'Uncle Felix *will* be annoyed, won't he? We were supposed to be safe from crimes here! Serve him right for treating us like children.'

So she is thinking along the same lines as I am, as usual.

While we wait for the policeman to stop marching about and decide what to do next, I will explain all the steps leading to the moment that the Detective Society came upon their seventh murder mystery.

2

Daisy and I might look like schoolgirls, but we have not been going to school very much lately. In January my grandfather, my Ah Yeh, died. Daisy and I had to leave Deepdean School for Girls (where we are fourth formers), and rush to my home in Hong Kong to mourn him. By the time we came back to England, after all the awful adventures we faced in Hong Kong, it was the beginning of May, and we had missed not just the spring term but the beginning of the summer one, too.

I was expecting to be sent straight back to school, but it was decided that we needed a rest after so much upsetting excitement in Hong Kong. We would not go back to Deepdean until the second half of term began on the first of June.

I thought that we would go to Fallingford, Daisy's house – but it was all shut up, as it usually is these days. Instead we were sent to London, to stay with Daisy's Uncle Felix and his new wife. We have been told to call the new Mrs Mountfitchet 'Aunt Lucy', and most of the time we remember.

Uncle Felix is just the same as he ever was, a fascinating and quite unnerving person, tall and golden like Daisy, and extremely clever too. He has a monocle that he has a habit of screwing into place over his eye and peering at me through, and he has an immensely important and secret job that we are not supposed to know anything about.

This job meant that, during the first week of our stay, he vanished for long stretches of time, returning quite unexpectedly to sweep us all out of the flat and into the glitter of London. He took us for afternoon tea at Brown's, to magic shows and the theatre, and for dinner shockingly late, at eight or nine at night, in restaurants where laughter sparkled off the golden walls, and ladies daringly showed their shoulders in evening gowns. We sipped Robinsons squash from champagne glasses, and I felt quite worldly.

While Uncle Felix was gone, though, we were left with Aunt Lucy. 'I shall be your governess,' she told us, mouth set firmly. 'I have had practice, after all, and work is . . . quiet at the moment.' Aunt Lucy's work, we have gathered, is almost as important as Uncle Felix's, and quite as secret.

I was expecting prim and proper instruction, like porridge for the mind. But I should not have been surprised that the lessons we were given turned out to be, once again, as unusual as Aunt Lucy herself. They were not like the starchy Deepdean hours of Latin and Deportment and the names of kings.

Just after we arrived, Aunt Lucy found the notebook full of codes I have been practising (and trying to make Daisy practise), and the next day my desk was filled with more code books than I had ever thought existed. 'Have a look at those,' said Aunt Lucy, 'and then begin to go through this exercise book. Solve what you can, and bring your work to me this afternoon.'

'Dull!' said Daisy, pushing them aside to perch on my desk – but I thought them quite marvellous. I lost myself in them for hours, far past the time I would have been brave enough to be seen studying anything at Deepdean, and only stopped when my brain was humming with numbers and symbols and languages.

Daisy, meanwhile, was given a set of lessons that was quite different. She was taken into another room in the flat, filled with racks and racks of clothes and hats and wigs and drawers full of make-up. After an hour or two, a wrinkly old lady with wispy white curls and a pair of thick spectacles, bent over in a shawl, came shuffling back out, Aunt Lucy following behind her. The old lady stood by my desk and in a creaky old voice said, 'Hazel Wong! I have a message for you!'

'I know it's you, Daisy,' I said to her. 'I can see your shoes are the same.'

'You wouldn't know if you met me on the street!' said the old lady in Daisy's voice. 'I do grant you the shoes though. Bother.'

Aunt Lucy smiled at me and said, 'Good eyes, Hazel. You're a natural. More practice needed, Daisy.'

Daisy sighed impatiently, but I could see she was thrilled by Aunt Lucy's unusual lessons – particularly because they were secret. There was an unspoken agreement between the three of us that Uncle Felix need not be informed about them. He is a very interesting uncle, but an uncle all the same, and he does not really approve of our detective adventures. Aunt Lucy, we could see, understood that being detectives was not a game. It was simply who we were.

Still, it was Uncle Felix who had the final say while we lived with him – and Uncle Felix continued to want us far away from murder or mystery of any kind.

And then George and Alexander came to visit for Daisy's birthday party, during their Exeat weekend. Daisy has written up the case that we solved at the British Museum, so I do not need to mention it here – apart from the fact that it was very exciting, and it made Uncle Felix more worried than ever about us putting ourselves in danger.

And *that* led to the reason why the Rue Theatre was suggested.

It was at breakfast on Monday morning, the eleventh of May, that we first heard of it. The maid, Bridget, had just brought in the toast and a pile of cryptic telegrams, neatly decoded in Bridget's clear handwriting. In Uncle Felix and Aunt Lucy's house, everyone seems to have an interesting and secretive life, and Bridget is an interesting and secretive maid who does far more than just the cooking and the cleaning.

Uncle Felix looked up from expertly slicing the bones out of a kipper and spoke to Aunt Lucy.

'I am glad you're with the girls again

this week,' he asked. 'They need a steady influence. The very word *aunt* sounds sensible. I'm sure you've become more staid since you became one, Lucy dear.' He winked at her over his kipper.

'That's nonsense!' said Daisy crossly. 'We don't need a steady anything!'

Uncle Felix avoided her glare.

Then Aunt Lucy put down the telegram she had been holding.

'That's a lovely sentiment, but I'm afraid I won't be able to oblige, Felix dear,' she said. 'Something urgent's come up at work.'

'What?' said Uncle Felix sharply. 'Nonsense, let me see!'

Wordlessly, Aunt Lucy handed him the telegram, and he read it.

'Good grief!' he said. 'How inconvenient. You're quite right. You'll be out all week.'

'Ooh, what's happened?' asked Daisy. 'Is it awful?'

'None of your business, niece,' said Uncle Felix. 'Lucy, what on earth shall we do? Could Bridget look after them?'

'I'm not a nursemaid, Mr M,' said Bridget from the doorway. 'And you know you asked me to watch those suspicious—'

'Yes, ahem, quite right, I did,' said Uncle Felix, frowning her into silence.

'We shall be quite all right on our own!' cried Daisy. 'We can explore London properly at last. How exciting!'

'You certainly shall NOT!' said Uncle Felix.

Aunt Lucy held up her hand.

'Wait,' she said. 'I have had a thought. Let me make a few telephone calls.'

She murmured something to Uncle Felix and then went out into the hall. Twenty minutes later, she was back, looking serene.

'Felix, dear, you want the girls to be watched over in an enclosed space, do you not?' she asked.

Uncle Felix nodded.

'And Daisy, you want excitement, don't you?'

'Naturally!' said Daisy.

'And Hazel, you love stories?'

'Yes?' I said cautiously.

'Well then,' said Aunt Lucy. 'I think I have found the perfect solution for everyone. One of the girls at work – her aunt is Frances Crompton, the owner of the Rue Theatre. Frances is putting on a new production of *Romeo and Juliet*, but with the flu that's going round this spring she keeps on losing actors. All of the usual bit part players have been snapped up by other theatres – they can afford to pay better, poor Frances is in a bit of a bind financially at the moment. Under the circumstances, I thought she might not mind looking after two temporary cast members – for a small fee, of course. And she agreed.'

'Lucy!' said Uncle Felix. 'Well – I suppose they'll be looked after there, at least.'

Daisy's eyes were widening, and she looked from Aunt Lucy to Uncle Felix and back again. 'What – *us*?' she asked. 'Not *really*?'

'Really, Daisy,' said Aunt Lucy. 'Have you heard of Frances Crompton?'

'Of *course* I have!' gasped Daisy. 'Why, she's famous! The Rue Theatre might be going through a difficult time, but it is still quite the most important Shakespearean playhouse in the country!'

'Excellent. So, how would you like to be in its new production?'

'To go on the stage!' cried Daisy rapturously, all her confusion and suspicion forgotten in a moment. 'Goodness, how marvellous! Isn't it marvellous, Hazel?'

'Oh,' I said, gulping. 'Oh, I . . .'

I can't think of anything worse was what I wanted to say, but I bit my tongue. Daisy looked so shiningly excited, and so I tried to ignore the roaring black gulf that had opened up in my stomach.

'I *thought* you'd be pleased, Daisy,' said Aunt Lucy. 'A bit part in *Romeo and Juliet*!'

'But Aunt Lucy, I shall not be a *bit part*,' said Daisy scornfully. 'I shall be the star.'

'Daisy dear, you could not be anything else,' said Uncle Felix. 'I suppose it is a neat solution for you. But what about Hazel?'

'I shall be all right,' I said, swallowing with difficulty.

'I quite agree, Hazel. You may not think yourself an actress, but I know better. You've been around Daisy for too long not to be able to pretend.'

'Rude!' cried Daisy. 'You've only been married to Uncle Felix for five months and you're already becoming far too much like him.'

Uncle Felix laughed, and smiled at me, and Aunt Lucy smiled too. And I wondered, at that moment, whether this was not another one of Aunt Lucy's unusual lessons.

I am still not sure. But whether it was supposed to be or not, that is why Daisy and I joined the Rue Theatre Company.

3

As Daisy, Bridget and I stood in front of the Rue Theatre after lunch the next day, I felt rather queasy, as though I was still on the boat that had brought us back from Hong Kong. I had been in agony all morning, while Daisy danced about the flat in raptures. I could not bear the thought that I would have to act – and in front of people!

But I had to admit that the theatre itself was a gloriously impressive place. The Rue is set to one side of a roundabout near Leicester Square, and it is a red-and-white brick cliff of a building, studded with shiny windows. It looks rather like a castle, and it even has four slender turrets shooting up the front of it like battlements. The noise of battle surrounds it too, for the roundabout in front of it sends up constant noise, all the howls of brakes and horns and shouts that are the sounds of London in a hurry.

London ought not to feel so different from Hong Kong, but it does. Although it is spring here, just as it was in Hong Kong, in London that means sun mixed up with chilly, windswept days, rushing grey skies and pattering rain, with only a few small sad flowers drooping in pots on windowsills. I miss Hong Kong's generous heat, its wide bright skies and blooming jungle. I even miss its spiders. And I miss the feeling of being at home. In Hong Kong I could breathe out, but now we are back in England, I have to go back to being wary. It is as though being in Hong Kong removed a layer of my skin, and now I have to grow it all over again.

But all the same, I am not quite as different in London as I am at Deepdean – or rather, there are more people here who are different like me. I have seen several faces on buses and in the London Underground just like our friends George and Harold, and even (my heart jumps with excitement every time) a few faces like mine.

As I was thinking all this, Bridget ushered us through the main doors of the Rue, and we found ourselves in a hallway that swept upwards in gold and black and red. It was empty, and there was a wonderful hush as the doors swung shut and cut off the noise from outside. Light glittered from chandeliers and shone darkly off marble, and the very air smelt warm and rich. At the sight of all that magnificence, Daisy expanded, eyes shining in the lights. I gasped. It was so beautiful, so magical – despite myself, I smiled.

'Now, remember what your aunt said,' Bridget told us firmly, her wide, freckled face and dark eyes frowning. 'Be on your best behaviour or, despite everything, Miss Crompton will send you straight back home. Is that clear?' Bridget is very no-nonsense. She says this is because she grew up in Dublin.

'Crystal,' said Daisy, rolling her eyes.

'*Best* behaviour, Daisy,' said Bridget, swatting at Daisy's shoulder. 'You shan't get anything past me.'

She winked at us both in a way that was clearly a warning, just as someone came down the stairs towards us.

She was wearing a shapeless brown dress, and she moved heavily, thumping her feet down on each step and squeezing the gold railing so hard I thought she might leave dents in the metal. She was old, older than even most of our mistresses at Deepdean, and her hair was grey and close-cropped. She was built as solidly as her footsteps and the round glasses that sat on her nose looked tiny in front of her large face.

'What are you three doing here?' she barked at us. 'We're closed, you know!'

'Good afternoon!' said Daisy, bobbing a curtsey. 'You're Miss Crompton, of course – I've seen your picture. We've come to be in your play.'

'Good afternoon,' said Bridget, standing up straight. 'I'm Bridget O'Connell. I believe you spoke to Mrs M on the telephone about these two girls?'

'Yes, all right, very good, but why are you *here*? This is the public entrance. Theresa left it unlocked in error. My actors go through the stage door, no exceptions. Do you think you are important?'

My heart sank. Miss Crompton did not seem very friendly.

Daisy blinked. 'We made a mistake,' she said, squaring her shoulders and standing as upright as she could next to Bridget. 'It won't happen again.'

Miss Crompton narrowed her eyes. 'It certainly won't,' she said. 'I was just coming to lock up – this entrance won't re-open until opening night itself. All right, girls, follow me if you please. Your aunt has arranged that you are to be in my play no matter how dreadful you are, but all the same I am curious to see what you are made of.'

I have been to plays before, and sat in the nice dusty darkness of the stalls, but I had never been on a stage until that day. I had not realized how very big a theatre is, the way the circles of seats rise up in front of you like mountains, the way the lights get in your eyes and the greasepaint smells get in your nose, the way your legs go wobbly and you want to sink through the floorboards and never be seen again. That day, standing on the vast empty stage alone, even my breaths seemed to echo around me.

'State your name!' boomed Miss Crompton from somewhere in the stalls.

'Er,' I said stupidly. 'Um . . .'

'Does not know her own name,' said Miss Crompton. 'Excellent. Begin your recitation, if you please.'

Daisy and I had discussed this, just in case we were asked to audition. I had spent the afternoon before learning a very sensible speech by Juliet's Nurse. Only, when I opened my mouth, I froze. The words slipped out of my mind, and all I could think of was part of *Ode to a Nightingale*.

'Thou wast not born for death, immortal bird!' I gabbled. It was such a schoolgirl thing to recite, a poem that everyone learns when they are little shrimps. 'Perhaps the self-same song that found a path through the sad heart of Ruth when, sick for home, she stood in tears amid the alien corn . . .'

Then, of course, I realized why I had chosen it – for I have often felt like Ruth in that poem, and I did at that very moment. I staggered on to the end of the poem, melting under the lights and frying with dreadful shame, for I had let out more of myself than I had meant. Then I stopped and there was only a ringing silence. I felt as though every empty chair were staring at me.

'Unique,' said Miss Crompton's voice from the stalls. I knew she did not mean it kindly. 'Off the stage, if you please. Next!'

I scrambled down the little set of steps at the right of the stage that led down into the audience as quickly as if the stage had tipped me off it. I sunk down into a plush seat next to Bridget, who was making deft squiggling notes in a small code book, just as Daisy came waltzing on. Safe in the stalls, I suddenly felt the dazzling excitement of the theatre again. The golden arch over the stage shone like a promise and the velvet darkness of the wings was heavy with the most thrilling mystery. In the middle of it all, Daisy seemed to glow. She stood with her hands clasped and her feet positioned as though she was about to do ballet, and she was beaming.

'Good afternoon!' she trilled. 'I am the *Honourable* Daisy Wells. May I begin?'

'You may,' said Miss Crompton – and did I imagine it, or was a chuckle in her voice?

Daisy threw herself into a kneeling position and reached forward. Her face changed to an anguished mask.

'What's here?' she cried. 'A cup, closed in my true love's hand? Poison, I see, hath been his timeless end . . . I will kiss thy lips!'

She leaned forward and a very small motion with her lips, as though she was being forced to kiss her Great Aunt Eustacia at Christmas. I tried not to giggle. Daisy and romance do not get on.

'O happy dagger!' screamed Daisy, leaping upright and waving her fist in the air. 'This is thy sheath, there rust and let me *die*!'

She plunged her hand into her stomach and doubled over, gasping. Then she slowly crumpled to the ground, making small whimpering noises, twitched twice and then lay still.

I waited. Bridget turned a page in her notebook and sighed to herself. At last, Daisy rolled over and opened her eyes.

'I'm all right really,' she said to Miss Crompton.

'I had guessed,' said Miss Crompton. 'Well, well. That was wonderfully tasteless. You clearly have no formal training and a very active imagination, but I commend your enthusiasm.'

'Thank you,' said Daisy, curtseying. 'Who will I be playing?'

Miss Crompton sighed. 'Since you are joining the Rue out of necessity, and at the request of your aunt, I shall make the most of the situation. You will be playing two small roles: Paris's Page, and also Rosaline. The second is a wordless part, of course, but both have great potential for drama.'

'Hmm,' said Daisy. 'I accept. What about Hazel? I can't possibly act without her, after all.'

'Miss Wong, are you *sure* you would like a part?' asked Miss Crompton. Without stopping her scribbling,

Bridget turned to stare at me, lips pursed. I wanted to sink down into my seat, but then I saw Daisy up on stage. Her arms were folded and she was trying to look commandingly at me, but she only succeeded in looking rather pleading.

Daisy had travelled halfway across the world for me, I thought. To me, stepping onto a stage felt almost as enormous. I decided that I could do it, and I would do it, for her.

So I swallowed down the rushing terror in my throat, and said, 'Yes. Please.'

Have you read them all?

Sign up to the Robin Stevens monthly newsletter for . . .

- Messages from Robin

- Exclusive extracts

- Activity sheets

- Bunbreak recipes

- Quizzes

- Up-to-date event information

- The chance to have your question answered by Robin!

Head to robin-stevens.co.uk/newsletter
to sign up, detectives!